AMAZING ANIMALS!

Adapted by Tisha Hamilton
Illustrated by Robbin Cuddy

SCHOLASTIC INC.

New York   Toronto   London   Auckland   Sydney
Mexico City   New Delhi   Hong Kong   Buenos Aires

ISBN 0-439-62748-6

10 9 8 7 6 5 4 3 2 1   04 05 06 07 08

Printed in **Mexico**
First printing, January 2004

Emily Elizabeth and her Big Red Dog, Clifford,
lived on Birdwell Island.
The carnival was in town, and Emily Elizabeth
went on rides with her friends Charley and Jetta.

Clifford enjoyed the great carnival food with his friends Cleo and T-Bone.

Everyone went to see Larry's Amazing Animal Show.
Larry Gablegobble announced each act.

Rodrigo the Chihuahua lifted weights — and dropped them. *Clunk!*

Dorothy the cow walked a tightrope. Shackelford the ferret flew off his trapeze swing, landed on Dorothy's head, and started to juggle.

A balloon floated up to Dorothy — and made her lose her balance. *Thunk!*

Dirk the Extreme Dachshund did stunts on his rocket skates — too fast. *Smash!*

Clifford, Cleo, and T-Bone thought the show was great! They went backstage afterward to meet the stars.

Shackelford the ferret peered up at Clifford, amazed by his giant size. "Do you want to join our cast?"

"Wow!" said Cleo. "I love showbiz!"

"We're entering a contest," said Shackelford. "The winners get fame, fortune, and a lifetime supply of Tummy Yummies."

"Thank you for your offer," replied Clifford, "but we can't come with you. Sorry."

"Well, here's the ad for the contest, anyway," said Shackelford. He gave it to Cleo.

The next morning, Emily Elizabeth brought Clifford his breakfast. Then she went back inside the house.

"Clifford has a big appetite," said Mr. Bleakman.

"Big?" Mr. Howard said with a smile. "It's huge!"

"That dog must eat you out of house and home," said Mr. Bleakman. "Feeding him must be a BIG problem!"

"Well, it isn't always easy," admitted Emily Elizabeth's father.

Clifford couldn't believe his ears. *I'm a big problem!* he thought. He ran out of the yard.

"But we don't mind," said Mrs. Howard. "We love Clifford."

"He's one of the family," said Mr. Howard.

Clifford couldn't hear them. He was already too far away.

"Is something wrong?" asked Cleo.

"I need to find a way to feed myself," Clifford told them. "I'll join Larry's Amazing Animal Show and win the lifetime supply of Tummy Yummies!"

He took Cleo's ad and hurried home.

That night, Clifford said good-bye to Emily Elizabeth without waking her up. Then he headed off to find the carnival.

Down by the beach, Cleo called out, "Not so fast, big guy!"

"We're going with you!" panted T-Bone.

"We'll come home as soon as we win the contest," promised Clifford.

In a city across the sea, the dogs soon found Larry's Amazing Animal Show.

All the animals welcomed them warmly.

"Welcome to the family," said Larry. "Now we really have a chance of winning the Tummy Yummies contest!"

Emily Elizabeth missed Clifford terribly and searched for him all over Birdwell Island. She and Charley found a giant paw print on the beach.

"I think the dogs left the island," said Emily Elizabeth. "But why?"

As the show traveled from city to city, the performers got better and better. Clifford helped a lot.

He helped Dorothy get over her fear of heights. He helped Rodrigo feel more sure of himself onstage. And he helped Dirk learn to control his skateboard.

They were ready for the big contest!

At the contest, Larry's Amazing Animals performed their stunts, and Clifford saved the show. The audience cheered! They especially loved Clifford.

Emily Elizabeth watched the Tummy Yummies contest on TV.
"And the winner is . . . Larry's Amazing Animal Show!" said
the announcer.
"Clifford!" shouted Emily Elizabeth.

Emily Elizabeth and her parents brought Clifford, T-Bone, and Cleo home.
Now they had enough Tummy Yummies to last a lifetime!
Clifford stepped in a puddle — and got mud all over Mr. Bleakman's car. *Splash!*

"Clifford!" shouted Mr. Bleakman. But then he smiled. "It's good to have you back, boy."

"Welcome home, Clifford," said Emily Elizabeth.
"Woof!" said Clifford. He had enjoyed his big adventure with Larry's Amazing Animal Show. But Clifford was happy to be back on Birdwell Island with all the family and friends he loved.